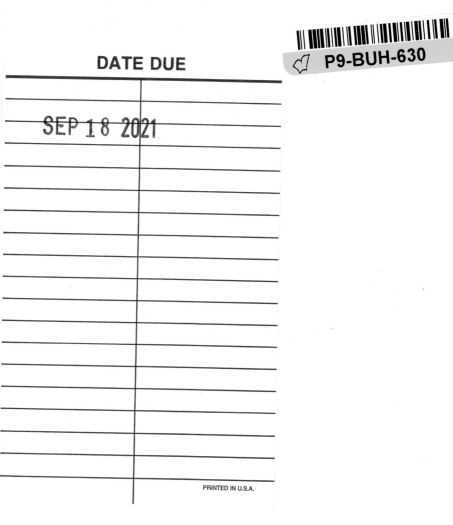

DATE DUE

SEP 18 2021

PRINTED IN U.S.A.

DELETE

P9-BUH-630

First Paperback Edition, November 2020   10 9 8 7 6 5 4 3 2 1

ISBN 978-1-368-07155-0
FAC-029261-20290
Library of Congress Control Number: 2020943688

Printed in the United States of America
Visit www.disneybooks.com

Disney Junior

Wash Your Hands!

Written by **Steve Behling**
Based on the series created by **Chris Nee**
"Wash Your Hands" song written by **Michelle Lewis** and **Kay Hanley**

Disney PRESS
Los Angeles • New York

FX: 05-21

"Good morning, Hallie!" Doc McStuffins says as she walks into the clinic.

"Good morning, Doc!" Hallie says. "What's first on your to-do list today?"

Doc says that before she does anything else, she's going to wash her hands.

"Why are you going to wash your hands?" Chilly asks. "Are you getting ready to eat?"

"Oh no, Chilly!" Doc says. "You just have to wash your hands to keep them clean."

"You see, there are little things called germs. They're so small, you can't see them," Doc explains. "Germs can make you sick. So it's a good idea to wash your hands! And the best way is to count to twenty while you are washing them to make sure they're clean."

"Oh, I get it," Hallie says.

"Can I try washing *my* hands?" Glo-Bo asks. "*All* of my hands?"

"Of course you can!" Doc says.

"I want to wash my hands!" Stuffy shouts.

"Me too!" Lambie says.

"You'll all get a chance!" Doc laughs.

As Glo-Bo starts to scrub his hands together, Doc sings a happy handwashing song!
"Wash your hands, wash your hands. Soapy-sudsy, wash your hands."

Glo-Bo makes sure to clean the fronts of his hands. Then he cleans the backs of his hands. He then washes in between his fingers, too!

Glo-Bo really likes washing his hands!

Now Doc helps Hallie wash *her* hands!
"You don't want to pass germs to your friends," Doc sings.
"Everybody wash your hands.
Soap and water, you can't go wrong.
Scrub as long as it takes to sing this song."

Glo-Bo had so much fun washing his own hands that he wants to help Squeakers get clean, too! He uses a toothbrush to give his friend a good scrub-a-dub-dub.

Next it's Chilly's turn! Chilly is a little worried about washing his hands, but Doc and Glo-Bo are there to help.

"Make them clean as they can get. Now dry them off and you're all set," Doc sings.

"Wash your hands, wash your hands."

Chilly realizes there is nothing to worry about. His hands are all clean now!

Surfer Girl wants to wash up, too. So Doc and Glo-Bo lend her a hand.

"Scrubbly-bubbly, wash your hands," Doc sings as Stuffy, Hallie, and Lambie join in.

"You don't want to pass germs to your friends! Everybody wash your hands," they all sing together.

"All together now! Everybody wash your hands."

"I know all about handwashing now," Chilly says. "What's the soap for, again?"

"Oh, Chilly." Doc chuckles. "You don't have to pretend to know everything. Let's go over it one more time."

"You use soap and water to wash the germs off your hands," Doc says. "You should scrub your hands all over for as long as it takes you to sing our handwashing song!"

Later that day, Doc finds Glo-Bo sitting outside at a play table.

"How are you doing?" Doc asks.

"Great!" Glo-Bo says. "I've been playing with paint all afternoon."

"All afternoon?" Doc says. "Can I see your hands, Glo-Bo?"

"Sure!" Glo-Bo says happily.

Then he shows his hands to Doc. They're covered in blue paint!

"I sure made a mess," Glo-Bo says.

But that's okay, because Glo-Bo knows exactly what to do!

Glo-Bo heads right over to Doc's clinic. He goes to the sink and turns on the water. Then he puts a little soap in his hands.

Next he starts to scrub!

Very soon Glo-Bo's hands are *nice and clean*. There's not even a trace of blue paint!

"I sure am glad I learned how to wash my hands," Glo-Bo says.

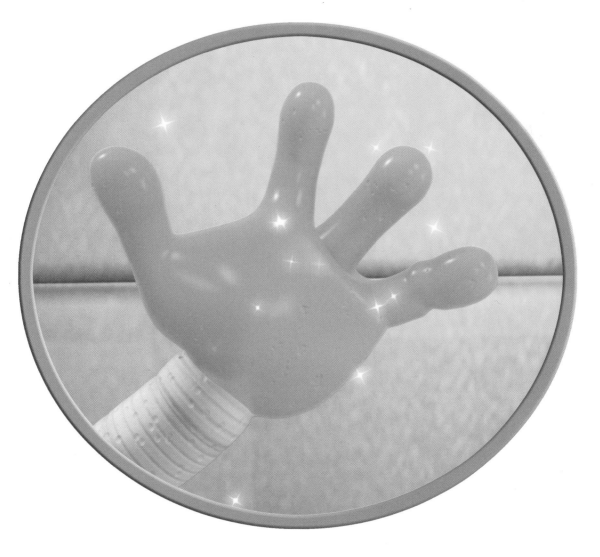

"And I sure am proud of you!" Doc says as she watches Glo-Bo. "I'm proud of everyone. I bet you all are going to do a great job of keeping your hands clean."

"You know it, Doc!" Hallie exclaims.

"I know I will," Stuffy says. "But, uh, just in case, do you think we could maybe sing that handwashing song again? Y'know, so I don't forget anything?"

Doc smiles. "Of course, Stuffy! Let's sing, everybody!"

Wash your hands,
     wash your hands.
Soapy-sudsy,
          wash your hands.
You don't want to pass
     germs to your friends.
Everybody wash your hands.

Soap and water, you can't go wrong.

Scrub as long as it takes
     to sing this song.

Make them clean as they can get.
Now dry them off and you're all set.
Wash your hands, wash your hands.
Scrubbly-bubbly, wash your hands.
You don't want to pass
germs to your friends.

Everybody wash your hands.

All together now!

Everybody wash your hands.

"Thanks again, Doc!" Glo-Bo says.

"You're welcome, Glo-Bo!" Doc says with a grin. "Just remember to wash your hands, and you'll be good to go!"